CONTENTS

TEENAGE MUTANT NINJA TURTLES™

ANNUAL 2005

Pedigree®

Published by Pedigree Books Limited
Beech Hill House, Walnut Gardens, Exeter, Devon EX4 4DH.
E-mail books@pedigreegroup.co.uk
Published 2004

£6.99

Meet the

TEENAGE MUTANT NINJA TURTLES™

SPLINTER ™

Master Splinter is the martial arts expert who rescued the Turtles as babies and brought them up as his own. He taught them in the ways of ninjutsu as soon as they were old enough, but also gave them the love and care they needed as they were growing up. The wise sensei is greatly respected by the Turtles – but he is also sometimes the target for their teenage pranks!

Leonardo ™

The 'big brother' of the Turtles is so dedicated to his training that the others call him Splinter Junior! Although he likes to take the lead, he's also a great team player and will take decisions based not on what is best for him, but rather what is best for the group. Leonardo's weapon of choice is twin katana swords and he has studied hard to become a skilled swordsturtle.

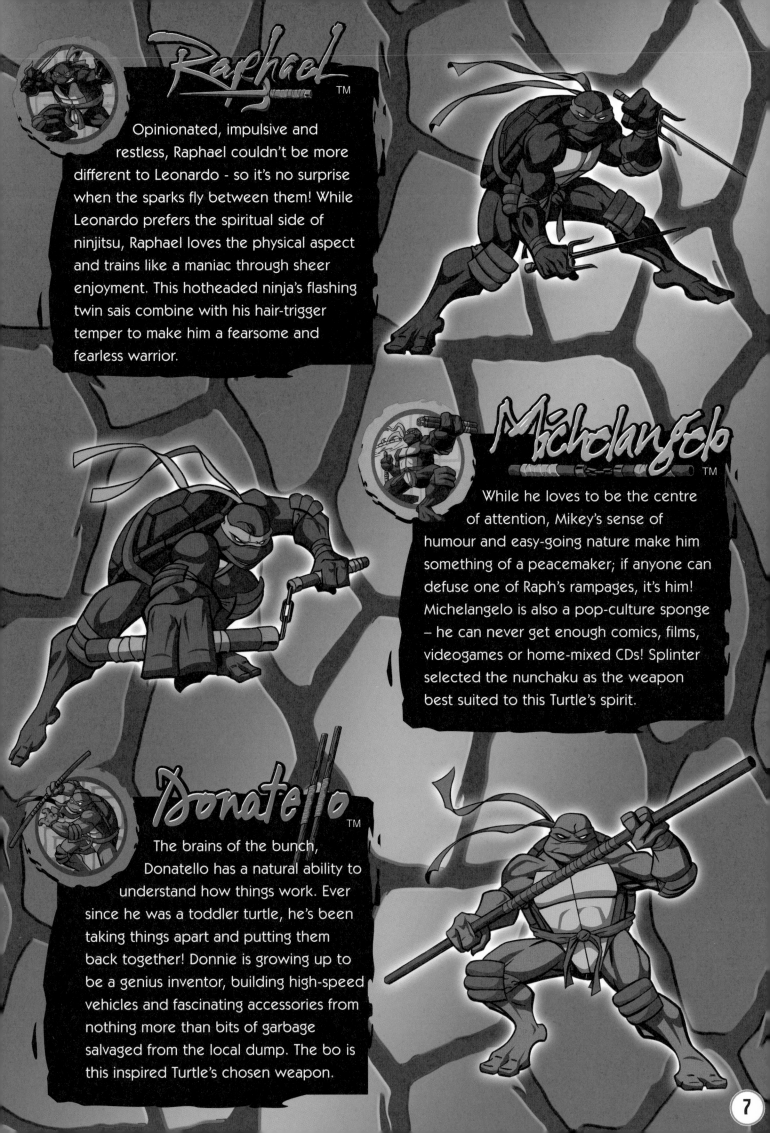

Raphael™

Opinionated, impulsive and restless, Raphael couldn't be more different to Leonardo - so it's no surprise when the sparks fly between them! While Leonardo prefers the spiritual side of ninjitsu, Raphael loves the physical aspect and trains like a maniac through sheer enjoyment. This hotheaded ninja's flashing twin sais combine with his hair-trigger temper to make him a fearsome and fearless warrior.

Michelangelo™

While he loves to be the centre of attention, Mikey's sense of humour and easy-going nature make him something of a peacemaker; if anyone can defuse one of Raph's rampages, it's him! Michelangelo is also a pop-culture sponge – he can never get enough comics, films, videogames or home-mixed CDs! Splinter selected the nunchaku as the weapon best suited to this Turtle's spirit.

Donatello™

The brains of the bunch, Donatello has a natural ability to understand how things work. Ever since he was a toddler turtle, he's been taking things apart and putting them back together! Donnie is growing up to be a genius inventor, building high-speed vehicles and fascinating accessories from nothing more than bits of garbage salvaged from the local dump. The bo is this inspired Turtle's chosen weapon.

SHREDDER ™

Oroku Saki is to all appearances a wealthy, respectable Japanese nobleman. However, his alter ego, the Shredder, is infamous throughout the underworld as a powerful and savage criminal. A true ninjitsu master, he has taken all that he has learnt of the ancient arts and used it for his own evil ends. One look at his multi-bladed armour explains how he got his name!

HUN ™

As a young street punk, Hun was spotted by the Shredder and chosen to become his lethal, loyal right-hand man. A massive mountain of solid muscle, he is also a skilled ninja and is The Shredder's first choice for the most important missions. Hun still bears the old scars of a ferocious bite from Splinter, who was trying to protect his beloved master, Yoshi.

FOOT ™

Based in New York City, the Foot is a global criminal organisation whose history, traditions and practices are based on the ways of Ninja. Led by the Shredder, the Foot's various divisions oversee every type of criminal activity, from local gang violence to corporate crime.

BAXTER STOCKMAN ™

Stockman, founder of the new technologies company Stocktronics, is a crazy inventor with ties to the Foot. A hero to the outside world, his rat-exterminating 'Mouser' robot earned him the respect of New York's citizens and media. What no one realises is that he plans to use these new inventions to tunnel into bank vaults and finance more evil schemes with the loot!

LEATHERHEAD ™

Leatherhead is a mutant crocodile who lurks deep in the sewers under New York City. He becomes embroiled in a battle with the Turtles when Michelangelo spots him by chance and discovers he is living in their old lair. Is he the ferocious reptile that he seems? You'll have to read 'What A Croc!' in this annual to find out!

In The Beginning, There was Ninjitsu...

I am Master Splinter, the sensei of the Teenage Mutant Ninja Turtles. It is I who trained them from a young age in the mysterious and powerful ways of the ninja. Before I tell the story of how my path crossed theirs some fifteen years ago, let us first go back a whole millennium to the birth of the art of ninjitsu…

Monkey Ninja!

Sarutobi (Monkey Jump) is just one famous ninja of legend. He was renowned for his superhuman acrobatic skills and it was said he lived in the trees, amongst monkeys.

This ancient martial art was created as a way of doing battle with the ruling Samurai elite in 11th Century Japan. Because it was illegal, knowledge of this secret culture was passed down the generations only by word of mouth. The ninja of legend were superhuman beings who possessed supernatural powers: they had the ability to disappear, walk on water, read minds and dodge the sword swipes of the swiftest warrior.

Young ninja were trained as early as possible, usually from the age of six of seven. This is the age my Turtles were when I began teaching them. A ninja's physical training is based on stealth, endurance and the expert handling of many types of weapons. Just as important is a ninja's mental preparation: a true ninja must be in control of his or her own mind. Add to this the mystical skills of legend and you have a ninja that is dangerous when empty-handed, deadly when armed.

No doubt you are wondering how I, a mere rat, became so knowledgeable in the ways of the ninja. I owe it all to my incredibly skilled master, Hamato Yoshi. It seems a lifetime ago now when I used to watch from my cage as he practised ninjitsu skills to perfection in his dojo. It's very painful for me to remember the fateful night when he was slain by the Shredder and Hun. I did my best to protect him, I bit Hun with all my might, but I was no match for the Shredder. Some way, somehow, I will avenge my beloved master...

I do not wish do dwell on that now. Needless to say, I made my escape and spent endless days wandering the streets. This was a strange new land for me and it was difficult, in my grief-stricken state, to survive. I had to search through the city's garbage for scraps of food and would sometimes take refuge in the sewers with the other rats. I gradually learned to fend for myself, but I was merely existing. I had lost everything. Then one day, when I was least expecting it, something happened on the streets of New York City that was to change my life, and that of four baby turtles, forever...

I was up on the streets, looking for my next meal, when I was startled by the screech of brakes. I turned to see a large truck veering unsteadily as it avoided a pedestrian, releasing a loose can from its load. The can bounced down the street towards the pet shop, where a boy was leaving with a bowl of four baby turtles. He didn't even see the can coming. It crashed into the bowl, smashing it on impact and releasing the turtles in a gush of water. The turtles were swept down into the sewer, along with the can. I knew the baby turtles would soon perish if left alone, so I scurried down into the sewer after them.

CAUT
MEN AT

14

The sewers are not the cleanest of places, but even I was shocked at what I saw when I caught up with the little turtles. The bouncing can had smashed open, emptying out a strange, green goo everywhere. This stuff even glowed - I had never seen anything like it! The turtles were paddling around in the lurid slime, happy as you like, and were completely covered in it. I sniffed around and found a coffee tin to gather them up in, then took them to my burrow to clean them up. I was soon to find out that this ooze had already taken effect and, of course, it had been impossible for me not to come in contact with it myself.

That night, with the baby turtles asleep and safe in their can, I felt something like happiness. I had always been part of Yoshi's happy family and since that terrible night, I had felt lonely for the first time in my life. Now I had a new family to care for.

When I went to see how the babies were the next morning, I was taken aback to find that the can had been tipped over. The four little turtles were scuttling around and what's more, they were now not so little: in only twenty four hours, they had doubled in size! It seemed that the mysterious goo had strangely affected their growth and I began to wonder what I had let myself in for.

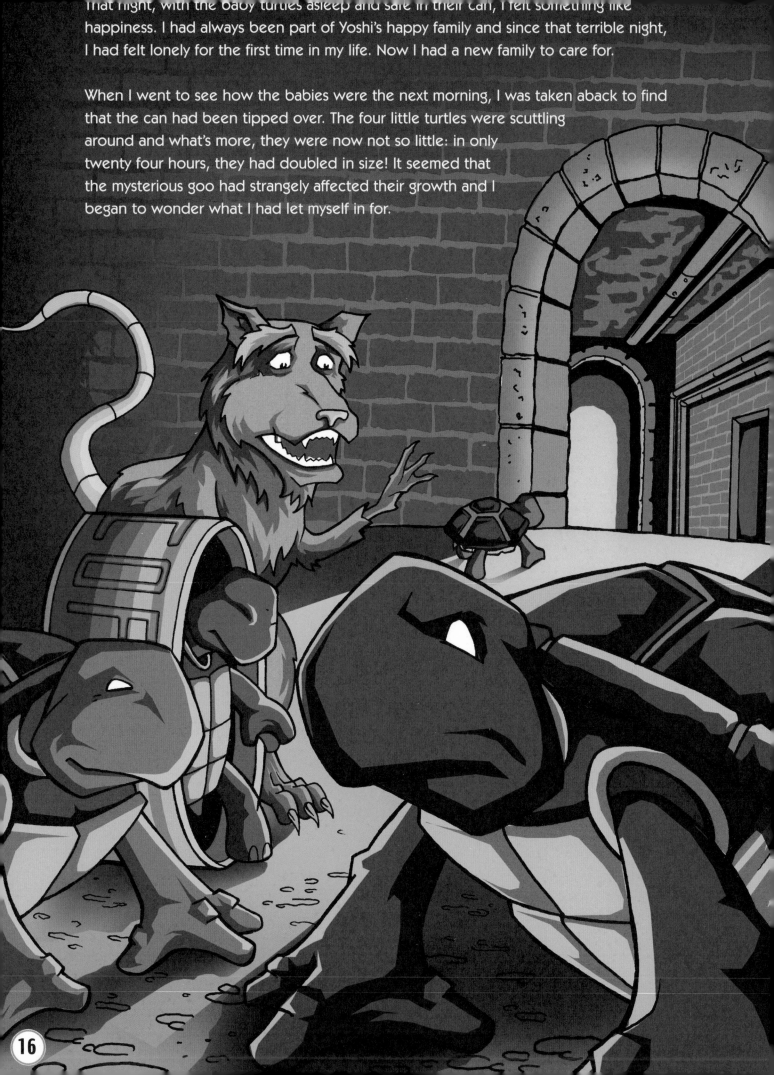

As the months went by, the turtles grew at a startling rate. Since I had come into contact with whatever it was that leaked from the can that day, I also became bigger. My mind became more active, my senses sharpened and with each day I felt stronger.

I was relieved when, at about a year old, my young turtles stopped growing. I became very protective and rarely let them out of my sight. My trips above ground had to be kept to a minimum; I could not risk their being discovered by anyone in the world at large. I had lost my family once and I would die before I let it happen again.

The intelligence of my turtles constantly amazed me. The memory of the day when they first spoke my name will stay with me forever. Many more words followed, as did the ability to walk upright and copy my movements.

I decided that as soon as they were old enough, I would begin to share with these unique creatures the martial arts expertise I had learned from watching Master Yoshi. They would need all the help they could get if they were to survive and prosper in the outside world as adults. They would need to be strong; they would need to be wise; they would need to be ninja!

Of course, it takes years to become a truly gifted ninja and even now my turtles still have much to learn. During those first years of training, though, they were model pupils and fast learners. They became wise, they acquired the art of stealth and they would practise endlessly to perfect their skill in the use of every new weapon.

Each of my turtles had his own personality and I could easily tell them apart. They still needed names, however. Having no idea what to call them, I rummaged amongst some garbage and looked in a discarded book on Renaissance art for inspiration. What names did I choose?

Meet . . .

Leo

Mikey

Don

Raph

20

WEAPON WORDSEARCH

Weapons training is a major part of ninjitsu and, as the Turtles will tell you, practice makes perfect! First, though, you have to know your weapons. Listed below are some of those a skilled ninja may use. See if you can find them all in the wordsearch square the words read up, down, backwards, forwards and diagonally.

SAI	BOW AND ARROWS	HANBO
BO	TESSEN	SICKLE
KATANA	DARTS	KAMA
NUNCHAKU	CHAIN	TANTO
SHURIKEN	SWORDS	YARI
POISON	ASHIKO	HOKO
SCYTHE	BOKKEN	KUNAI
BATTLEAXE	FUKIYA	ONO
CHIGIRIKI	JO	

S	W	O	R	R	A	D	N	A	W	O	B
H	I	J	P	O	I	S	O	N	Y	T	A
U	R	C	H	S	D	R	O	W	S	N	T
R	A	M	K	C	H	A	I	N	A	E	T
I	Y	C	A	L	T	A	N	T	O	S	L
K	I	S	M	H	E	T	A	G	P	S	E
E	K	M	A	N	E	K	K	O	B	E	A
N	U	N	C	H	A	K	U	O	J	T	X
B	F	Z	T	O	J	H	A	N	B	O	E
I	W	Y	L	K	J	S	T	R	A	D	H
A	C	O	N	O	K	I	H	S	A	I	O
S	P	C	H	I	G	I	R	I	K	I	B

QUICK ON THE DRAW

Michelangelo is a real comic-book freak and even sketches his own super-hero stories! He loves to draw his brothers, too. Grab a pencil and he'll show you how to draw a really cool dude in four easy stages!

1

2

3

4

Piece o' Pizza!

If the Turtles get the munchies, there's a good chance they'll go for pizza – WITHOUT ANCHOVIES! If Master Splinter's making a big one to share, he has to do four different toppings to make sure each Turtle gets his fave!

Get creative with your own pizzas and try lots of different toppings. Take a pizza base, slap on some pizza tomato sauce, choose your toppings, then ask Mum to bake it for you – and don't forget to say thanks!

Super stars!

Use biscuit cutters to make the cheese into wacky shapes – stars look great!

Fruitadelic!

Pineapple's not the only fruit you can have on a pizza. Most fruits go with cheese, especially grapes and apple, so slice 'em up and throw 'em on!

Smile!

Use your toppings to make a face – Pepperoni for eyes, a mushroom slice for a nose, ham strips or peppers for a smiley mouth and sweetcorn or cheese for crazy hair! Can you guess whose face is on the pizza?

Sweet pizza!

Why not try a pizza pudding? Use jam instead of tomato sauce, add some fruit, then grate some chocolate to sprinkle on top so it goes all melty in the oven. Eat with ice-cream or cream for a delish dessert!

Rebel Reflections

Hothead Raphael loves the physical part of training!
Look at this picture of him practising his ninja moves
and say which of the pictures below is his reflection.
The answer is at the bottom of the page.

1

2

3

4

5

6

GHOST SHIP

Science, maths, logic and rationality, dudes. Those are the things that order my world. Things that can be proven. Things that make sense.
Donatello here, with a story that I wouldn't believe if I hadn't experienced it myself!

It was Halloween and close to midnight. New York City was enshrouded in fog – a fog so dense that you couldn't see beyond a couple of metres. Perfect ninja weather!

My three brothers – Leonardo, Michelangelo, Raphael -- and I were walking along one of the city's abandoned piers.

We could smell the sandy mud-flats below us, a sharp pungent mix of decaying seaweed, rotting fish and motor oil. The tide must have been out.

"Pee-yu!" said Michelangelo. "That smells almost as bad as Hun's breath. Almost."

"Never mind that," cut in Raphael. "Look out across the bay, in the moonlight that's beginning to spread across the water…."

The four of us stopped to look. It was the silhouette of a ship. Not a tanker or a fishing boat like the ones commonly seen around New York but a ship with large billowing sails. And it was coming straight towards us!

Within moments the ship grounded itself on the tidal flat about one hundred metres to our right.

"Change in plan," announced Raphael, leaping off the pier in the direction of the ship.

"Turtle overboard!" yelled Michelangelo as the rest of us leapt after Raphael.

"It's weathered and old... a derelict ship," observed Raphael.

"Look at the cute girl," said Michelangelo, pointing to the prow of the ship and its figurehead carved in the shape of a woman.

"It's English," I said, "late fifteenth century from the looks of it. But these types of ships haven't been around for hundreds of years!" I knew this for a fact -- maritime history is one of my favorite studies.

"It's awesome!" said Michelangelo as he began to pull himself up one of the many ropes hanging down from the sides of the ship.

The three of us scrambled after him, pulling ourselves up onto the ship's planked deck.

"Look, a door!" exclaimed Michelangelo, racing across the deck.

Michelangelo pushed open the door, stepped into the room and promptly froze in his tracks.

"You guys aren't going to believe this!" he yelled.

The four of us crowded into the room. Across from us stood a large wooden chest, shut tight by a large iron padlock. Beyond the chest a dozen or so human skeletons lay across the floor, cutlasses and various swords scattered amongst their bones.

"A pirate ship!" Michelangelo yelled gleefully. "A real pirate ship! With a real treasure chest!"

He ran to the chest and began tugging on the padlock.

"Locked tight!" he announced. "Hey, Raph, gimme one of your sais so I can jimmy open this padlock. Michelangelo began working Raphael's sai like a crowbar against the padlock.

Kneeling amongst the bones I saw that the various weapons were of different origin. Most were English, while others were Spanish, Portuguese and Persian. A mixed crew. Maybe these were pirates after all.

Something sparkled at the periphery of my vision. An old bottle with a note sticking out of it.

"What's the note say?" asked Leonardo.

"It's pretty faded," I said, "but it looks like it says 'Lift the curse… by freeing the lady… and letting the sands of time…."

Snap! went the padlock as it broke open.

"…wash over her," I finished. "Lift the curse by freeing the lady and letting the sands of time wash over her.' That's all it says."

"I got a bad feeling about this," stated Leonardo.

"Gimme a hand with this lid, Raph," said Michelangelo. Together they heaved the old wooden chest open.

Whooosh! went the air escaping from the opened chest.

But it wasn't just air… it was glowing air. And it didn't just escape, it rushed out of the opened chest towards the skeletons.

"I got a bad feeling about this," repeated Leonardo.

"Nuts!" exclaimed Michelangelo, looking inside the chest, "it's empty! No pirate booty!"

Raphael stiffened. "Um, Mikey," he ventured, "I don't think it was empty. I think you might've freed the souls that were locked within."

"Souls? Whose souls?" asked Michelangelo, dreams of pirate riches fading from his thoughts.

"Their souls!" scowled Leonardo, unsheathing his two katana swords and motioning towards the skeletons.

For the skeletons themselves were now beginning to glow. Worse, they were beginning to move. Pulling themselves together into semblances of men. Arm bones to shoulder bones. Wrist bones to arm bones. Finger bones to… weapons.

The skeletons began to stand.

"Wow," said Michelangelo, awestruck. "Pirate skeletons! How cool is this?"

"Not cool, bonehead," Leonardo hissed at Michelangelo.

"Speaking of boneheads," said Raphael, "these dudes don't look too friendly!"

The skeletons began to walk stiffly towards us, skulls grinning, clenched fists raising ancient weapons.

Weapons at the ready, brothers," ordered Leonardo.

Michelangelo tossed Raphael the sai he had used to open the padlock before pulling out and defensively spinning his pair of nunchaku in the air. Raphael plucked the tossed sai out of the air with his left hand, bringing it down parallel with the sai in his right hand. I withdrew the bo staff from behind my back and pointed one end at an approaching skeleton.

"This can't be happening. Skeletons don't just wake up from the dead," I said. The skeleton closest to me suddenly lunged forward. I gave its skull three quick raps with my bo, knocking it aside. The raps sounded hollow.

"Well, it is," said Leonardo, backing away towards the open cabin door as he crossed swords with a very tall skeleton. Sparks flew as their weapons struck.

"We need more room to fight," he said, "let's take this out onto the deck."

The fog outside had increased since we had entered the cabin but shafts of moonlight shone through here and there illuminating the last thing we wanted to see: more skeletons!

"There must have been more crewmen below deck," guessed Leonardo. One of his katana flashed in the moonlight. A skull went flying over the deck.

Over to one side I watched as Raphael used the fog to his advantage, hiding within it and sneaking up behind a skeleton that wielded two Spanish cutlasses. I was surprised to see that Raph had sheathed both sais.

"Excuse me," Raphael said to the skeleton, as he tapped it on its right shoulder, "but I got a bone to pick with you." With his other hand he gripped the skeleton's right humerus bone and pulled it free.

The skeleton took no notice and simply attacked Raphael with its left arm.

"How do they do this?" he asked. "How do they parry our moves if they don't even have eyes with which to see us?"

"Maybe stakes need to be driven through their hearts… or maybe we need to shoot them with silver bullets," offered Michelangelo, leaping over one skeleton and smashing another to bits with a nunchaku.

"You know, something supernatural," he added, disarming another skeleton by wrapping a nunchaku chain around its left radius and ulna bones and yanking it free at the elbow. Its forearm clattered to the ground.

"I follow your point, Mikey," said Leonardo as he fenced with two short skeletons simultaneously. "We have to fight fire with fire. And you're right, this is supernatural." Leonardo fought his way towards my side. Bones flew about in the moonlight.

"That note," he said to me, "there was something about a curse. How'd it go again, Donnie?" I thought about it. " 'Lift the curse—'" I began, only to be interrupted by Raphael.

"The curse must refer to these skeletons," he said.

"The curse of being trapped aboard a ghost ship," added Michelangelo.

"But there aren't any such things as ghosts or ghost ships!" I countered, cracking a skeleton hard and loud upside its head as I spoke.

"Just because science can't explain the supernatural doesn't mean it doesn't exist," said Leonardo. He threw a skull towards me. As if for emphasis its teeth chomped and chattered like a joke shop gift.

If I couldn't apply science, then I would apply logic. Maybe my brothers were right. Perhaps I could find some logic to these seemingly supernatural events. I thought again about the old note and turned towards Leonardo.

" 'Lift the curse by freeing—' oof!" But I didn't have a chance to finish the recitation – a skeleton had tackled my legs from behind and began pushing me towards the deck's railing!

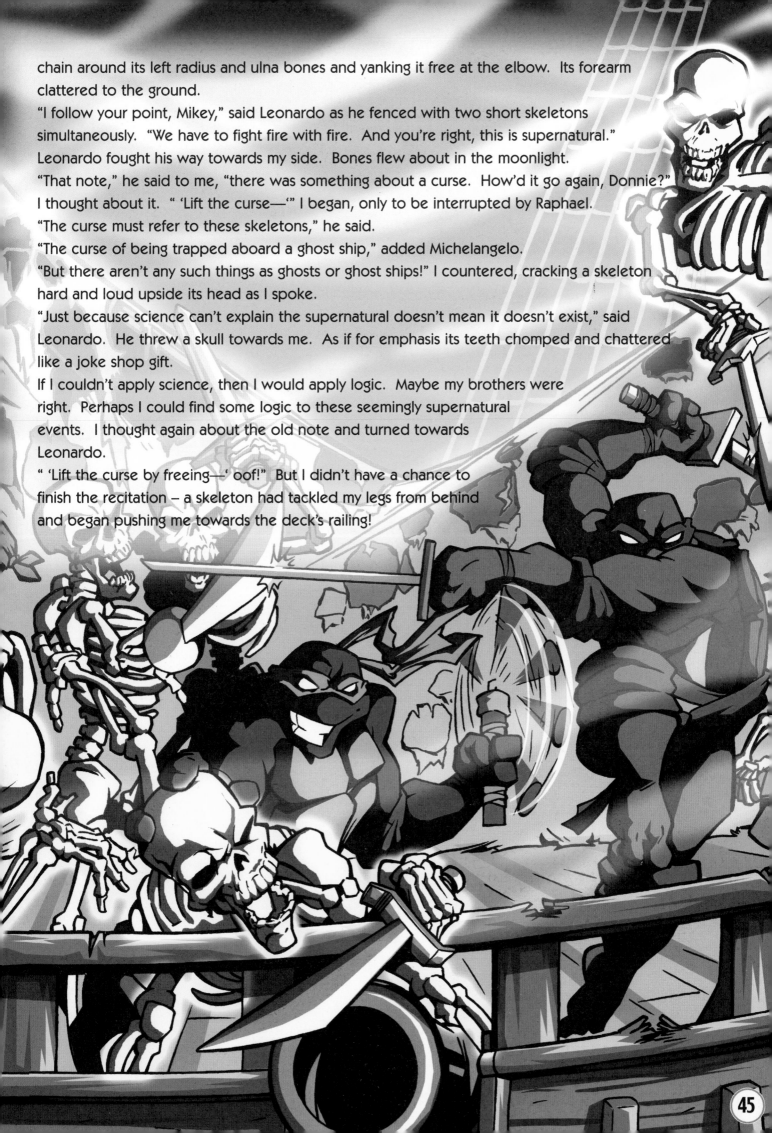

Over the railing I sailed, the skeleton holding fast to my legs. Because I went over back-first there was a brief moment where I caught sight of the deck above me. Two other skeletons jumped over the side in pursuit. One had its cutlass gripped between its teeth in true pirate fashion.

Sha-muck! came the sound of my shell impacting the marshy tidal flat. Not only did I get the wind knocked out of me but I was stuck fast in the muck. Looking up I saw the two other skeletons land nearby. Three of them in total. And me, stuck in the mud!

All I could do was go on the defensive. I spun my bo staff around like a helicopter's blades and was able to dislodge the skeleton that had been holding on to my legs. But the others kept hacking at my bo with their swords, wearing me down. I looked past them for a moment and caught sight of the ship's figurehead of the woman.

The woman. The lady.

Lift the curse by freeing the lady....

Of course! The note must be referring to the figurehead!

Thwack! went the sound of my bo staff as it was struck with enough force to send it flying out of my grip.

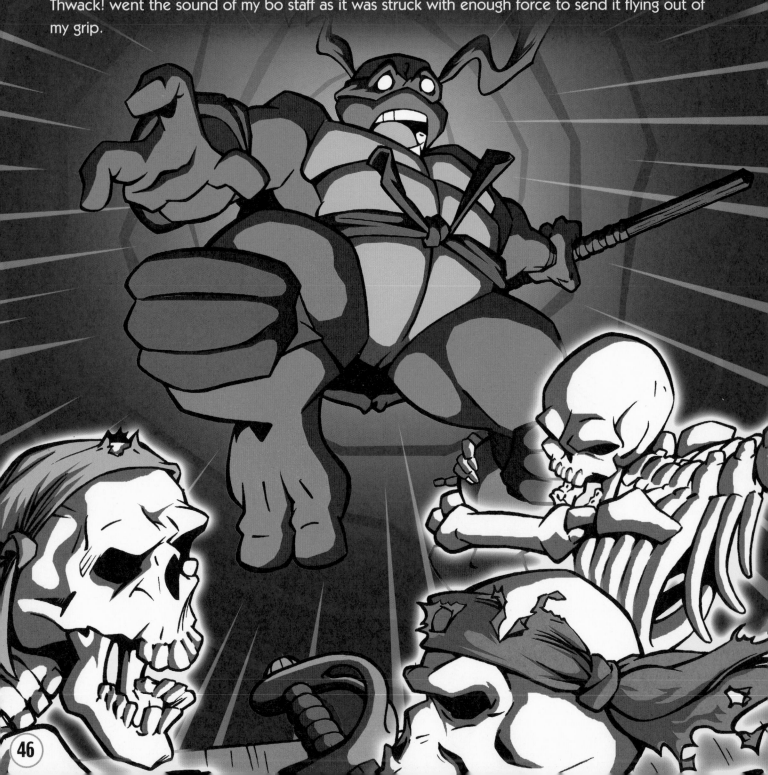

Suddenly I was defenseless! I had the answer to the curse but I was defenseless!

The three skeletons looked down at me and began to raise their weapons in unison when a sudden blur of motion swept them away with a shattering blow – it was Raphael, swinging by on one of the ship's overhanging ropes!

The next thing I knew I was being pulled to my feet.

"Don't mention it," said Raphael.

"Th-thanks, bro," I stammered and then blurted out: " 'Lift the curse by freeing the lady…'" that lady." I pointed to the ship's figurehead.

"Right on," grinned Raphael in understanding. He called up through the fog to Leonardo in a loud voice. There came a hacking sound, then a splintering crack followed by a loud SHMUCK! as the figurehead fell onto the tidal flat.

"How'd the rest of that note go?" asked Raphael, looking up towards the ship where we could still hear the sounds of battle.

" 'Lift the curse by freeing the lady… and letting the sands of time wash over her,'" I answered.

"Hmmm, I dunno," said Raphael.

I felt something touch my foot. Water. The tide was beginning to come in. The tide. Of course!

I think I got it," I said. "Here, help me bury her here by the water's edge…."

Together, we began to dig in the soft sandy muck.

"… by the water line, where the ebb and flow of the tides will always wash over her," I continued.

"The sands of time? I get it. I sure hope you're right, Donnie," said Raphael, pushing muck atop the figurine. All that was left showing was its head.

As soon as I covered it over completely there came a great crumbling sound and two loud splashes from where the ship had stood but was now no more.

The two splashes were Leo and Mike falling into the bay as the ship disappeared out from under their feet. They soon swam to shore and rejoined Raph and me. The four of us looked at one another in silence, then looked at where the ship had been. It was gone, as were the skeleton pirates. Off in the foggy distance of the city a church's bells rang twelve times.

Midnight. Halloween. A curse lifted. A good deed done. Even if it was outside the realm of science!

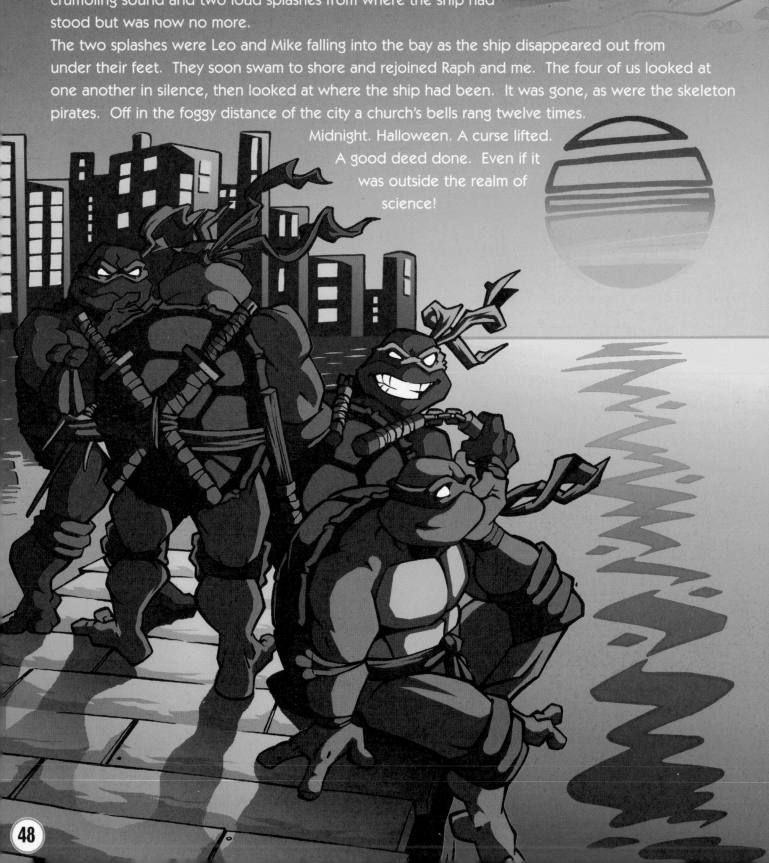

SEWER SEARCH

Uh-oh! Mikey's in trouble deep down in the sewers! Show his brothers which way to go so they can apply some Turtle whacks to help him out, but watch out for loony Baxter Stockman!

Which Weapon?

See if you've been paying attention and can match each Turtle to his weapon of choice. No peeking at the answers or flicking through the pages, now!

Sai

Bo

Katana

Nunchaku

Of course, a true ninja is trained to be a master of all weapons. Read on to see how this skill comes in handy at times…

Answers: Leonardo – Katana, Raphael – Sai, Michelangelo – Nunchaku, Donatello – Bo.

WHAT A CROC

SSSPPYIAAAH!

GET THE OTHERS!

WHAT IN THE SHELL...?!

EVERYTHING SEEMS NORMAL DOWN IN THE SEWERS. MICHELANGELO IS CARRYING OUT ROUTINE UNDERWATER REPAIRS, WHEN SUDDENLY...

THE OTHERS ARE SOON ON THE SCENE...

SO I WAS, LIKE, WHOAH, AND THIS CROC THING WAS ALL GRRRRR, SO I'M LIKE GUGUGUG, THEN IT GOT ALLRWWWOARR AND IT WAS, LIKE, GRRRRWWWRR WITH THE CLAWS...

A MONSTER IN THE SEWER? YEAH, RIGHT!

CUCKOO!

CRAZY!

LOOKS LIKE YOU'RE ONE RIB SHORT OF A BARBECUE, BRO'!

LOOK, I KNOW WHAT I SAW. THERE'S A HUGE, UGLY REPTILE IN THE SEWERS... AND FOR ONCE IT'S NOT YOU, RAPH!

I'LL PROVE THIS THING EXISTS AND I'LL PROVE IT NOW!

HAVE THIS PORPOISE DEVICE, MIKEY. IT'S GOT A BUILT-IN CAMERA, TRANSMITTER AND TWO-WAY RADIO. IF YOU SEE THE...THING, SO WILL WE.

STAY TUNED, GUYS, AS MIKEY TV TAKES YOU ON A CROC HUNT!

WHATEVER.

MICHELANGELO SOON SPOTS THE CROC...

EUREKA! THE CHASE IS ON!

WHERE THE CROC GOES, MICHELANGELO FOLLOWS...

ARE YOU GETTING THIS, GUYS? HE'S IN OUR OLD LAIR!

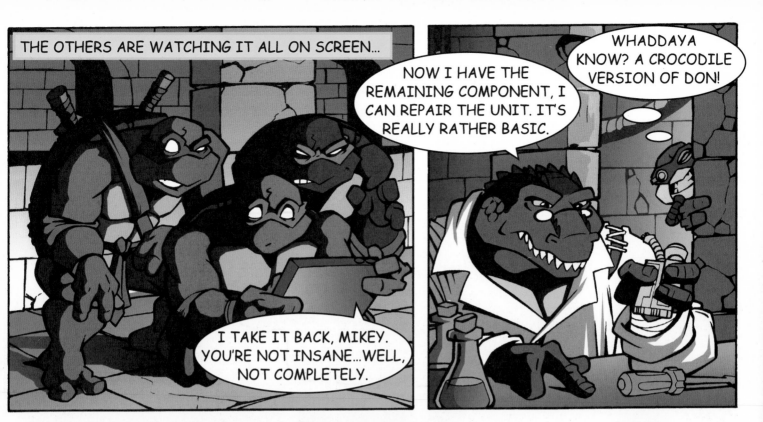

THE OTHERS ARE WATCHING IT ALL ON SCREEN...

NOW I HAVE THE REMAINING COMPONENT, I CAN REPAIR THE UNIT. IT'S REALLY RATHER BASIC.

WHADDAYA KNOW? A CROCODILE VERSION OF DON!

I TAKE IT BACK, MIKEY. YOU'RE NOT INSANE...WELL, NOT COMPLETELY.

SUDDENLY, MIKEY IS SPOTTED!

AN INTRUDER?

OKAY, TIME TO GO!

GRRNNCH!

ROOOWAARR!

YIIAAAH!

"...THEY SAVED ME FROM THE SEWERS WHEN I WAS CAST THERE BY A HUMAN. WHILE THEY KEPT ME FOR OBSERVATION, I WAS EXPOSED TO A POWERFUL MUTAGEN THEY HAD INVENTED..."

...I BECAME PHYSICALLY AND INTELLECTUALLY POWERFUL, ACCEPTED BY THE UTROMS AS PART OF THEIR FAMILY. BUT THE HUMANS CAME TO DESTROY US...AND I WAS LEFT BEHIND WHEN MY FAMILY ESCAPED."

BUT WHEN I FINISH BUILDING THIS TRANSMAT, I WILL JOIN THEM ONCE AGAIN.

BUT WHO'S THIS?

AH, MY FRIEND HAS RETURNED. GENTLEMAN, ALLOW ME TO INTRODUCE YOU TO...

BAXTER STOCKMAN!

OH, LEATHER HEAD. IT WAS THESE TURTLES THAT SABOTAGED THE TCRI BUILDING, DESTROYING THE TRANSMAT AND MAKING YOUR FAMILY LEAVE!

BAXTER STOCKMAN TELLING LIES? IMAGINE THAT!

THEM? THEY ARE THE TRAITORS?

NNGGRRNN!

YES! YES! THEM! THEM!

NOW WE CAN PUT THE YOU-KNOW-WHAT TO WORK!

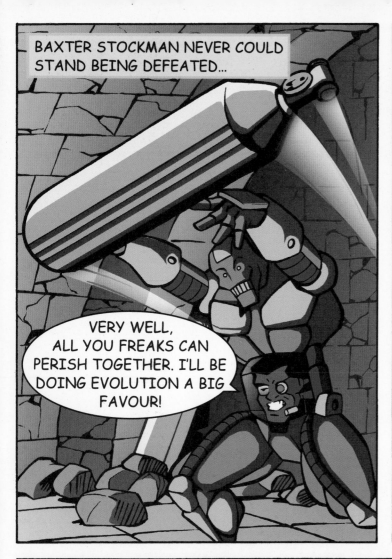

BAXTER STOCKMAN NEVER COULD STAND BEING DEFEATED...

VERY WELL, ALL YOU FREAKS CAN PERISH TOGETHER. I'LL BE DOING EVOLUTION A BIG FAVOUR!

BOOOM!

NO!

LEATHER HEAD! COME WITH US! FORGET ABOUT THE TRANSMAT!

NO. HE BETRAYED ME. IF I CANNOT HAVE THE TRANSMAT ...IF I CANNOT GET BACK TO MY FAMILY...LIFE IS MEANINGLESS. LEAVE ME.

MIKEY! MOVE IT!

MICHELANGELO IS FORCED TO LEAVE LEATHERHEAD BEHIND...

CRASH!

SMASH!

61